Katie Woo

Keep Dancing, Katie

by Fran Manushkin

illustrated by Tammie Lyon

PICTURE WINDOW BOOKS
a capstone imprint

Katie Woo is published by Picture Window Books
a Capstone Imprint
1710 Roe Crest Drive
North Mankato, Minnesota 56003
www.capstonepub.com

Library of Congress Cataloging-in-Publication Data
Manushkin, Fran, author.
  Keep dancing, Katie / by Fran Manushkin; illustrated by Tammie Lyon.
    pages cm. — (Katie Woo)
  Summary: Katie loves being the best dancer in her dance class, so
when Mattie joins the class and begins to outshine her, Katie is jealous.
  ISBN 978-1-4795-5187-3 (hardcover) — ISBN 978-1-4795-5189-7 (pbk.)
  ISBN 978-1-4795-6156-8 (eBook)
1. Woo, Katie (Fictitious character)—Juvenile fiction. 2. Chinese
American children—Juvenile fiction. 3. Dance—Juvenile fiction.
4. Jealousy—Juvenile fiction. [1. Chinese Americans—Fiction. 2. Dance—
Fiction. 3. Jealousy—Fiction.] I. Lyon, Tammie, illustrator. II. Title.
III. Series: Manushkin, Fran. Katie Woo.

PZ7.M3195Kd 2014
813.54—dc23   2013048929

Art Director: Heather Kindseth Wutschke
Graphic Designer: Kristi Carlson

Photo Credits:
Greg Holch, pg. 26
Tammie Lyon, pg. 26

Printed in the United States of America in Stevens Point, Wisconsin
122015   009399R

DISCARD

Table of Contents

Chapter 1

Dance Class

Katie loved to dance.

She and JoJo were in a class together.

Katie bragged, "I'm a fabulous dancer!"

"I'm not a great dancer,"
said JoJo. "But that's okay.
I love to dance. It makes me
happy."

One day,

Miss Kelly said,

"Class, I have

some good

news. In a

few weeks, we

are having a

show."

"Yay!" shouted Katie. "It's

fun dancing on the stage!"

JoJo asked,
"What music
will we use?"

"'You Are My
Sunshine,'" said
Miss Kelly.

"I love that
song," said Katie. She leaped
high. She spun fast. Nobody
could dance like Katie.

Then a new girl joined the class. Her name was Mattie.

At first, Katie liked her, but not for long.

Mattie jumped higher than Katie. She could spin faster, too.

It made Katie sad. She told JoJo, "I'm not the best anymore."

"Don't be sad," said JoJo. "You are still terrific!"

Chapter 2

Ready for the Show

Miss Kelly played, "You are my sunshine, my only sunshine."

It was such a happy song. Mattie smiled as she danced.

Katie did not.

"Oops!" said JoJo. "I keep falling down."

"That's okay," said Miss Kelly. "The important thing is to keep dancing. Just do the best you can."

Mattie showed JoJo how

to dance without falling.

JoJo was getting better.

She had a great time.

Katie did not.

Finally,
it was time
for the show.
"I don't feel
well," Katie
said.

"You look fine," said her
mom. "I know you will be
terrific today."

"I'm not so sure," Katie
sighed.

JoJo and Mattie were very

excited. "This will be fun,"

said Mattie.

But then —

"Uh-oh," said Mattie, looking worried. "I can't find my ballet shoes!"

Chapter 3
"Lost" Shoes

Katie saw the shoes. They were under a backpack.

"Hmm," thought Katie. "If Mattie can't find her shoes, she can't dance. Then I'll be the best again."

Katie sat on top of the backpack.

Mattie searched for her shoes. JoJo helped her. They searched and searched.

"Oh, Katie," said JoJo, "have you seen Mattie's shoes?"

"Um, no," said Katie.

JoJo looked hard at Katie.

Katie looked away.

Mattie began to cry. Katie tried to look away, but she couldn't.

"I feel stinky," she said. "*Very* stinky."

It was not a fun feeling.

Katie jumped up, saying,

"Mattie! I found your shoes."

"Thank you!" said Mattie.

"I wasn't going to tell

you," confessed Katie.

"But you did," said JoJo.

"And I'm glad." Katie

smiled.

Katie and JoJo and Mattie

hurried to the stage. Katie

leaped high. Katie spun fast.

It was her best dancing

ever.

She and JoJo and Mattie
held hands as they took a
bow. The audience clapped
and cheered, so they took
another bow.

"You were all terrific," said Miss Kelly. "I'm proud of you!"

Katie felt proud, too. She sang "You Are My Sunshine" all the way home.

About the Author

Fran Manushkin is the author of many popular picture books, including *Baby, Come Out!*; *Latkes and Applesauce: A Hanukkah Story*; *The Tushy Book*; *The Belly Book*; and *Big Girl Panties*. There is a real Katie Woo — she's Fran's great-niece — but she never gets in half the trouble of the Katie Woo in the books. Fran writes on her beloved Mac computer in New York City, without the help of her two naughty cats, Chaim and Goldy.

About the Illustrator

Tammie Lyon began her love for drawing at a young age while sitting at the kitchen table with her dad. She continued her love of art and eventually attended the Columbus College of Art and Design, where she earned a bachelor's degree in fine art. After a brief career as a professional ballet dancer, she decided to devote herself full time to illustration. Today she lives with her husband, Lee, in Cincinnati, Ohio. Her dogs, Gus and Dudley, keep her company as she works in her studio.

Glossary

audience (AW-dee-uhnss)—the people who watch or listen to a performance, speech, or movie

ballet (BAL-lay)—a style dance with set movements

confessed (Kuhn-FESSD)—to admit that you have done something wrong

fabulous (FAB-yuh-luhss)—wonderful

sighed (SYED)—breathed out deeply, often to express sadness or relief

stinky (STING-kee)—very bad or dishonest

terrific (tuh-RIF-ik)—very good or excellent

Discussion Questions

1. Mattie was the new girl at dance. How does it feel to be the only new person at school or in a class?

2. Katie was jealous of Mattie's dancing. Talk about a time you felt jealous.

3. After Katie lies about Mattie's shoes, she says that she feels stinky. What do you think that means?

Writing Prompts

1. Katie loves dancing. Write about something you love to do.

2. If you could do a dance to any song, what song would you choose and why?

3. Mattie helps JoJo with her dancing. Describe a time you helped a friend.

Having Fun with Katie Woo!

After a wonderful dance show, it's nice to have a little party, and cupcakes make the best party food! You can make cute cupcake toppers using cupcake papers. Here's how:

Tutu Toppers

What you need for each topper:

• 1 cupcake liner

• 1 straw cut to 4 inches long

• card stock that matches the liners

• glue

• tape

• optional: stickers, markers, etc.

What you do:

1. For each topper, fold the cupcake liner in half. Then cut a small half circle to make the waist opening of the tutu.

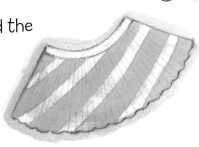

2. Using the leotard in the illustration on the opposite page as an example, cut a leotard shape from your card stock. You can ask a grown-up for help, because this is a little tricky!

3. Glue the cupcake liner to the leotard. Decorate your leotard and tutu with drawings or stickers.

4. Tape the leotard onto a straw. Now it's ready to be stuck in a freshly baked cupcake. Yum!

Download and print a sheet of ready-to-cut leotard shapes at:

www.capstonekids.com/characters/Katie-Woo

THE FUN DOESN'T STOP HERE!

Discover more at www.capstonekids.com

- ♥ Videos & Contests
- ✿ Games & Puzzles
- ♥ Friends & Favorites
- ✿ Authors & Illustrators

Find cool websites and more books like this one at www.facthound.com. Just type in the Book ID: **9781479551873** and you're ready to go!